SKIDDING
Sideways

Skidding Sideways
Copyright © 2025 JH Nelson

This new adult contemporary romance is recommended for readers 18+ due to mature content.

Cover design by 1231 Publishing

ISBN: 978-0-6451315-6-7

First Edition – November 2025

Published by J. H. Nelson

TO MY READERS

Thank you for all your ongoing support and heartfelt messages of encouragement and love for my stories and characters. It is so touching to hear that you all enjoy reading about my fictional friends as much as I do.

To my beautiful and talented team of word-genius friends and beta readers... Thank you for all your ongoing help, advice and cheering me on from behind the scenes. Without you, I would not be where I am today. I love you guys.

Skidding Sideways is a standalone companion novella to Dangerous Thrills. They share the same fictional world but feature different couples.

Enjoy!

ONE

———

Seeing the number on the screen, a sinking feeling hit Tom in the gut, but he tried to sound optimistic. "Hi, Mrs J. What can I do for you?" How he managed the positive lilt in his voice, he wasn't sure. What was it this time… he didn't know. The only thing Tom *did* know was that Mrs Jones never rang *just to chat*.

"Tommy. They've got him! I don't know where. I didn't know who else to call. I've left a message for John, but he isn't answering! I don't know what to do, Tommy."

"Slow down, Mrs J. Tell me exactly what happened." Tom snatched the grimy notebook from beside the monitor. Yanking his pen from his shirt, he began scribbling madly.

It took Tom less than five minutes to hand over the day's instructions to his employee, grab a couple of tools and his keys. With the baseball bat in the boot, he fled the workshop in a cloud of smoke and noise.

Of course, he couldn't be certain where Reece was holding his best friend captive, but having all grown up together, Tom was fairly sure he could find them. He had to. *Where are you, Pete? Where has that psychopath taken you?* Tom shook off his scattered thoughts. He needed to concentrate and keep a clear head.

Scouring the river docks, Tom saw a strange shape as he passed one of the oversized roller doors. Slamming on his brakes, he reversed and spun the car to highlight the area with his headlights. There, tied to an old office chair, was a beaten and bloodied Peter. His head lolled to the side lifelessly.

Bursting into action, Tom grabbed the bat and ran towards his friend. His emotions warred between dread for his friend's life and burning rage to kill the man responsible. Clinging to the bat with a white-knuckled grip, Tom spun around in search of Reece and his disciples. They were alone. *Cowards!*

"Pete? Come on, bud, open your eyes!" Tom cradled Peter's head. When Peter opened one eye— the other swollen shut—and attempted to smile,

Tom breathed the smallest sigh of relief. He was alive.

"Not gonna lie. It's bloody good to see you." Peter's words came out in a string of mumbles through his distorted face.

Tom choked out a laugh as he roughly swiped his eyes. "I wish I could say the same. You're a banged-up mess. Shit! Let me get you out of this."

Tom pulled his Leatherman from the pouch on his belt and began freeing his friend.

TWO

"That's really great news, Mrs J. Thanks for letting me know. He, uh, he clams up and changes the subject every time I ask him, so I appreciate you keeping me in the know. Yeah. Okay. Call me if you need any help getting him home. Bye."

As Tommy hung up his call, a young lady walked through the front glass door of the shop. 'Lady' seemed like a stretch. She barely looked like she was out of high school, the petite little thing that she was.

"Can I help you?"

"I'm hoping so. My car just crapped itself back down the road a bit." She thumbed over her shoulder.

"Well, if you can limp it over, I'm happy to take a look at it for you." Tommy wiped his hands on a dirty rag from behind the counter.

"Are you serious? You can't help me? I know nothing about cars, and to be completely honest... I can't afford to fix anything else on that piece of shit if I fuck it further by *limping* it over here! Thanks anyway!" The girl turned to leave, pushing the door open with enough force to send it flying.

What the hell? Fiery little thing.

Tom sighed and rolled his eyes. He knew he was likely to regret it, but something about her pulled at his conscience. Was it the lack of money he could relate to? Was it the thought of her being stranded in a dodgy industrial area? He didn't know. Against his better judgement, he raced out through the workshop. "Back soon, bud. Gonna go help this lady."

"Hey, wait up, love—" Tom stalled when she spun on him. The saying 'if looks could kill' came to mind, but now that they were out in the sun, Tom noted the delicate blue of her eyes for the first time. She was beautiful.

"Oh... now you want to call me love? Well, I don't think so, *darl!*" She emphasised the last word, snapping him out of his thoughts.

"Yo, bumblebee… Do you want my help or not?" Tommy exclaimed.

He watched the woman clench and unclench her fists. With an exaggerated sigh, she gave in. She nodded in defeat and turned to lead the way.

"What's your name, anyway? I didn't catch it between all your hissing back there," Tommy asked, a smirk on his face.

As he'd expected, the comment riled her and earned him a scowl of menacing proportions. He couldn't help his amusement, smiling. When he thought she might even stomp her foot petulantly, she relented instead.

"Lauren. And yours?"

"Tommy." He pointed to the embroidered name on his uniform.

"This is it." Lauren pointed to a small hatchback parked on the roadside. The paintwork on its roof needed respraying, but other than that, the car looked to be in reasonable condition.

"The keys?" Tommy held out his hand.

Folding his bulky frame into the small vehicle took effort, and he felt self-conscious in front of the beautiful young brunette. As Lauren climbed in the passenger seat beside him, their elbows touched, sending a spark of heat rushing up and into

Tommy's chest. *What the...?* Shaking off the thought, he returned to business. "So, tell me what it was doing? Did it actually stop, or did it go into limp mode?" He turned the key, lighting up the dashboard. To his trained eye, nothing immediately stood out as being a standard problem, and with multiple lights lit up, it could be anything. He'd need to explore it more thoroughly back at the shop.

In silence, they rode the short distance back. Tommy was in 'mechanic mode,' listening for any telltale engine noises. Even though his concentration was on the car, Lauren's closeness distracted him. She smelled amazing, like a tropical goddess of summer fruits and coconut. The scent filled his nostrils in the warm car from the mid-afternoon sun. It was strong, but undeniably feminine. He'd never been one to believe in that hocus pocus baloney, but somehow, he could *feel* her energy surrounding him in the small space, and it was unnerving. He needed to escape.

"Any ideas?" her voice startled him, scattering his far-off thoughts.

"Um. In short... no. I'll need to inspect it further, but for that, I'd need it for the rest of the afternoon at least."

"Any clue what this is likely to cost me?" She gnawed on her lower lip, and Tommy wondered if it was a nervous habit of hers.

"Tell you what... I'll look at it. *If* I find something quick and easy, well then, I won't charge you for any labour. But if I have to go exploring further, I'll call you beforehand, with prices. That way, there're no surprises, and you can decide if you want me to go ahead. Deal?"

"Yeah? Thanks. I really appreciate that."

"Too easy. Come on through to the office and I'll grab some details off you. You got a partner? Someone who can come and give you a lift?" Tommy held the door open for her to pass before himself. Again, he was struck by the odd zinging sensation that passed in air between them. *Pull yourself together, idiot! Be professional!*

"Oh. Um. Not really. Am I not allowed to wait here in the office? On that customer couch?" She pointed to the two-seater sofa pressed against the wall of the small office. "Oh, please excuse me a sec. I need to get this." She touched Tom's arm briefly, answering with her other. "Hello. Mum?"

Tom stood awkwardly at the computer behind the reception counter. He tried to focus on drafting a quote for another customer but found himself distracted—or was it intrigued—by her conversation.

"How's Dad?"

Silence. Tom watched her head drop. A frown creased her forehead, and he wondered what was wrong with her father.

"Yeah, I know, Ma. Me? Well, I'm actually at a mechanic. My car broke down." Tom reverted his eyes back to his screen when she lifted her head. "No, Ma, I don't need any money. I'll figure it out, okay? I don't want you to worry. You just worry about you, and Dad. Say hello to him for me? Love you, Mum. Bye." Tom watched her disconnect the call and stare at the blank screen a few seconds longer. He hadn't meant to eavesdrop, but the office was a small space, and with no one else in it, it was quiet enough that he'd heard her every word.

"So… is there really no one who can come and get you? You could be here for hours, is all. That will be very uncomfortable for you after any length of time. Trust me. No family? Or a friend even?" Tommy fiddled with the pen he'd retrieved from his breast pocket.

"My family live out west, so I don't really have anyone I can call on. I have a lecture I need to catch up on though, so I'm pretty content to just camp out here with my laptop, if that's cool?"

"Okay by me. What are you studying?" Tom immediately regretted asking, feeling awkward again. "Sorry, that's none of my business." He shuffled from one foot to the other.

"No, it's fine." She smiled. "I'm doing psychology. Still a long way to go yet, though."

Tom's eyes bulged, and she laughed at him.

THREE

Opening the heavy workshop roller door, Tommy noted the already steamy air as it rushed out against his face. It was going to be another scorcher. Thinking of the daily jobs ahead of him, Tom's eyes drifted to the back corner of the shed. Lauren's little car sat in the shadow where it had for the past four days. He hadn't been able to shake the memory of her since he'd given her a lift home the day they first met.

Together in his work ute, sitting in front of her apartment building, the two of them had swapped numbers so they could discuss the future of her little car once Tom had identified the problem. Lauren texted him the following morning to thank him again for what he was doing to help her out, and they'd been texting ever since. Their conversations had quickly shifted gears, and what started out as discussions about necessary repairs had transitioned into general chatter. Tom couldn't understand why a beautiful and intelligent twenty-three-year-old woman wanted to talk to a twenty-nine-year-old grease monkey like him, but her texts had fast become the highlight of his days.

Tommy was so busy at work that he couldn't understand how this beautiful stranger had wrapped a noose around all of his thoughts and held them hostage. Business was always hectic at this time of year, and with only one employee—Jack—plus himself, the pair were barely keeping up with the load. Tommy thanked his stars for the work. It was a good problem to have, but without enough hands, it was a problem, nonetheless. With Christmas only weeks away, Tom was giving Jack a paid week off between Christmas and New Year's. He deserved it. He'd been working his arse off for months without complaint. Tommy, however, would have to work through… he still needed to earn the money to pay for his goodwill gesture.

Away from work, Tom's best friend Pete was finally back on his feet, and that caused Tom stress, knowing those bastards would likely hunt him down again to finish what they started. Tommy rubbed his sternum. *Can you physically feel a stomach ulcer growing? Is that normal?*

He shook his head. His thoughts were all over the place. Customers would soon start arriving to drop off their vehicles, and he needed to get his brain into work mode. Jack arrived then, too. The pair prioritised their day and got to it, working alongside each other in the blistering heat.

It was almost lunchtime when Jack interrupted Tom. "Hey, boss. I've just finished that lady's car you requested. Just needs a quick test drive to make sure it's all running smoothly, and then it's good to go. You want me to take it out? Or you wanna do it?"

"Nuh, I'll take it for a spin in a sec. Thanks, mate."

The news felt bittersweet. Tom now had a reason to call Lauren, where he would hear her voice again, but it meant her car was ready. And then what? Would they stop texting? Would she drift away into nothingness? Without her car's repairs glueing them together, he would have no reason to see or talk to her once she drove away. The idea made his insides twist. He couldn't get her out of his mind no matter how hard he tried. She wasn't the average customer.

He smiled, remembering their fiery introduction. He'd not seen any hostility from her since that first day. In truth, she'd been nothing but sweet and almost shy during their more recent discussions. He remembered the feeling of her presence pressing in on his entire being as they'd sat together. First, in her cramped little hatchback for the less than two-minute drive to his workshop and then when he drove her home in his company ute. Collecting her keys from the office, Tommy headed out to take the hatchback for a test drive. As he climbed into the driver's seat, cute girly figurines stared at him from their globs of Blu-Tack along the dashboard. A lip balm and a pen lay in a small compartment beneath her radio. Tom imagined her climbing into the same seat a million times or more. Sparks zinged along his arms, being in her private space.

FOUR

Despite the chaotic pace of the day, Tommy's mind never stopped turning over. He was tightening a bolt when the idea struck him. The answer to his workload issue had been right in front of him the whole time. He was excited to move forward with his plan.

The other 'plan' he'd decided on… he wasn't nearly as confident about.

After phoning Lauren earlier that day about her car being ready, Tommy had offered to pick her up and drive her back to the shop. He'd pointed out that catching public transport during peak hour would be a nightmare for her. Reluctantly, she'd agreed.

Tommy checked his watch for the umpteenth time. He wished he could stop off at home first to freshen up before seeing her again, but that would look suspicious given she knew he'd been at work all day.

With the day's jobs completed and customers gone, Tommy all but pushed Jack out the large roller door under the pretence of 'locking up'. The moment the roller door touched the concrete, Tommy whipped off his shirt and headed for the washbasin. With the blackened bar of soap from all the greasy hands it had cleaned, Tommy lathered and rinsed his face, neck and pits in an effort to freshen up. Having worked in the stifling shed on a forty-degree December day, even *he* could smell himself. He grabbed the can of deodorant that he kept on his desk for days such as this and gave himself a generous spray before jumping in the truck. His heart picked up speed as he headed for her house.

Lauren was waiting in front of her unit complex when Tom turned onto her street. He took a steadying breath as he pulled over, smiling at her through the windshield before she climbed in.

"Hi," he said, a little too enthusiastically. He was acting weird. He knew it. He just hoped she didn't notice. *Get a hold of yourself, man!* He adjusted the revision mirror for something to do.

"Hi." She gave him a quick smile. "Thanks again for doing this. I can't thank you enough."

Tommy nodded, and with the flick of his wrist, indicated back out onto the street.

"All part of the service," he joked, smiling. "Hey, do you mind if we make a quick detour? My place is only two streets over, and I have to grab a folder for work. I meant to grab it this morning, but of course I forgot." He rolled his eyes, still annoyed at his mistake.

"Ah. Yeah. Sure."

Tommy looked at her. Was that worry he heard in her voice? Thinking about it properly, it made sense. Here she was, a beautiful young woman from the country with no family close by, putting her trust in a complete stranger. It wouldn't be the first time his lumberjack build and thick, bushy beard had put people on edge. *Of course she's scared. Idiot.* "You know what… it's fine. I should've realised how sus that would sound. Especially to a woman. Sorry." He shook his head and bit his tongue to stop babbling.

"No, it's fine." She assured him. "Truly. You've been so generous and gone out of your way to help me with my car, dropped me home and now picked me up as well, to go collect it. I don't want to put you out any further. Please… go get your folder.

I'll just wait in the truck—" Lauren's stomach took that moment to interrupt with a loud gurgling sound. Tommy looked over in time to take in Lauren's wide, horrified eyes as a bright shade of red crept up her neck. She buried her face in her hands. "Oh, my god! I'm so embarrassed. That was my stomach, just so we're clear." They both laughed.

With her body angled away and her face still buried in her hands, Tommy let his eyes roam over her. She was a petite little thing. Tonight she wore a thin strappy singlet top that hugged her skin. He followed the curve of her spine down to the thin and inviting strip of bare back that sat between where her top ended and the waist of her denim cutoffs began. Heat stirred in his veins, and he adjusted himself discreetly. God… to run his fingers along that strip. To feel that skin at the small of her back, so tantalisingly close to her shapely rear end.

The arousal in his shorts grew uncomfortable. He stressed, knowing he would absolutely die of embarrassment if she saw the *tent* situation he had going on. *Get it together, man!* He shuffled in his seat to hide his growing predicament. He needed a distraction.

"Sooo, can I safely assume that you're hungry?" Tom teased.

"Well, I'm not sure I can deny it at this point." Lauren laughed at herself. "I skipped lunch in favour of finishing my assignment. But hey, at least it's done now."

Tommy pulled the truck up in front of his house. He left the engine running so the air conditioning would keep the cab at a comfortable temperature for her.

"Okay, this might be too forward, especially given your hesitation to be alone with me just now, but... I'm hungry too. Maybe we could grab a bite to eat after I get these forms? Have a think about it. I'll be right back."

Before she could reply, Tommy leapt out and jogged up the front stairs of his high-set house. Only when he reached the top and unlocked the door, did he sneak a glance back at her before disappearing inside.

The moment he stepped inside, Tom's brain went crazy with all the reasons why he should've kept his mouth shut. Why he shouldn't have asked her to dinner. What was he thinking? She was young. Beautiful. Not the type of girl who'd ever want to go out with a guy like him. And what about him? Was it honestly a good idea for him to want a woman who's studying psychology? Wasn't that a conflict of interest or something? He had enough shit going on without worrying if she was analysing his every move like some weird social experiment. Tom muttered to himself and grabbed the document folder.

Heading back to the car, Tommy wasn't sure if the uneasy feeling in his stomach was from hunger, nerves, or both, but he hoped it settled down soon. He felt nauseous, and the fear of vomiting in Lauren's presence only made the sick sensation worse.

Climbing back into the truck, Tommy welcomed the cool air that hit his skin. What he hadn't counted on was the assault on his senses from her delicious-smelling perfume. Like a tropical pool-side cocktail, that he wanted to soak her up all night long.

He needed to keep his mind straight. There was no way this beautiful and intelligent little bumblebee would ever be interested in a no-good, greasy, high school dropout with a shady past and extensive rap sheet. *Don't forget 'fat, useless and disappointing excuse for a son'.* He felt the sting of his father's cutting words as he had so many times before.

Unable to bear Lauren's rejection, Tommy didn't ask and instead drove towards the workshop.

"So… where are we eating?" Lauren turned her entire body to face him, leaning into her corner of the truck cab.

"I don't know. Maybe it's not such a good idea," he muttered with little conviction.

"Why the change of heart?" Lauren squinted at him quizzically. "Did you scoff food while you were in there and now you're not hungry? Did you not think to share?" she teased.

Before Tommy could reply, however, he noticed the scowl creasing her beautiful brow. "What?" he worried.

"Wait. Are you ditching me for a better offer? A date or a girlfriend?"

Her nostrils flared, reminding Tom instantly of their first meeting. As much as he liked the friendly interactions they'd shared since then, it was the feisty bumblebee he'd first met that had kept him tossing and turning through the nights.

"What? God, no! You couldn't be further from the truth. It's nothing like that." He scratched the beard along his jaw.

"Well, then… what's the problem?" Lauren challenged, one eyebrow raised.

"Nothing. I just… I thought maybe it wasn't a good idea." He turned to her, imploring. "Five minutes ago you were nervous to be alone with me in the car… so I hardly want to push you into or make you feel any more uncomfortable or anxious by taking you to dinner as well." His eyes left the road again as he braved another glimpse of her. He was curious to read her face. Her thoughts.

She offered him a gentle smile. "That was just my mum's voice in my head for a moment. She's the eternal pessimist, and every now and then, her negativity creeps into my psyche. I think we should absolutely get dinner together. Unless… you *do* genuinely have somewhere else you need to or would rather be?" she asked.

"Heavens, no. I could totally eat. Where do you want to go?"

"Hm. It's a little out of the way, but have you heard about the new burger place that's opened up in the cafe precinct near the shopping centre? I hear it is supposed to be amazing."

"No, I haven't tried it. I've heard good things about it, though. My brother has been there, and he's been raving about it ever since."

"Sweet. Wanna give it a go?"

"Sounds like a good plan." Tommy smiled and stole another admiring glimpse of her beautiful body when her eyes followed something beyond the window.

FIVE

Leading a limping Peter through the workshop, Tommy found Jack. "Hey Jack, this is Pete. Pete, this is Jack. You've already kind of met in passing, I realise. Pete's going to be joining us and helping take some of the load off around here. He's recovering from… an injury, so he might be a little slow out of the gate, but I promise, he's worth the wait." Tommy turned to Pete, a look in his eyes.

Tommy still couldn't believe he hadn't come up with the idea sooner. The answer to his staffing issues had been right in front of him, without him realising. Pete working for him also meant that Tommy could look out for him and hopefully try to keep him safe from Reece and his gang. He owed him that much, and then some.

Tommy left the two men to get acquainted while he went to attack the overgrown pile of paperwork on his desk upstairs. Reaching the basic, undercoated office door on the mezzanine level, he opened it, catching the briefest relief from the broken and barely working air conditioning. Sadly, the mezzanine level, being so close to the tin roof, was the hottest area of the whole place. When Tommy had started up the business two years ago, he'd immediately installed the cooling unit. What he hadn't taken into consideration was how hard it would need to work, and the one he'd bought wasn't enough to cope with the extreme temperatures. One day, he would put in a better one. *One day.*

Tommy sat at his modest desk in his worn-out old office chair. The pile of papers overwhelmed him. He pulled out his phone instead and sent a text to Lauren.

Hi there. I'm avoiding paperwork. Tell me what exciting things you are doing right now, so I can live vicariously through you.

He put the phone down beside him and, with a groan, grabbed the first paper from the pile. Tom hated the clerical side of running his own business. He was on his fifth sheet when his phone pinged with a message. His heart did a double beat at the sound of it. *Jesus, get a grip, Tom… You're how old?*

Feeling stupid, Tommy snatched up the phone to read it.

Hi! Agh… want to swap? I am trying to finish my xmas shopping. My sister is so impossible to buy for, and I don't know what she does and doesn't have anymore, making it even harder these days. Have you done your xmas shopping yet? Are you one of those people who have everything organised nice and early, so you don't have to stress last minute?

Tommy chuckled. He was avoiding doing paperwork… did she honestly think he was the type to have Christmas shopping under control? Surely not.

I can't believe you're even asking me this. I am one hundred percent a 'Christmas Eve rush job' person.

He watched the speech bubble dots work across the screen. The anticipation of her next message had him sitting up straighter.

Oh, thank god I'm not the only one! The shops are crazy here today. I think I'm going to have to admit defeat and just gift card it for her. I need to go home. My feet are killing me, and I really should *be working on my uni essay. So, other than the paperwork… how is your day going?*

Tommy leaned back in his chair, thinking about her question. He remembered how she'd looked sitting across from him the night at the restaurant. The way she'd laughed over something he said, causing a chip to fall out of her mouth, making them both laugh harder. The pale blue of her eyes, ringed by their mesmerising dark blue outer circle. Other women undoubtedly envied her beauty. Standing beside her, Tommy couldn't miss the size difference between them. He was a heavyset man, tall enough to look mostly proportionate, but he'd never felt comfortable with his bulky appearance. The difference between him and Lauren had never been more pronounced than that night, when they'd stood together at the counter and he'd dwarfed her tiny frame.

A car in the workshop below revved, pulling Tommy back to the present. He blinked and returned to his phone.

It's pretty good. I've just hired a friend of mine to help around the shop, so hopefully I can start leaving this place at a reasonable hour each night.

Once sent, Tommy questioned what he'd written. Why did he tell her he was hoping to leave on time more often? Did he do it subconsciously because he wanted her to know he would soon be available in the evenings? Was it an over-share or too heavy to be considered 'casual' texting conversation? *You're such a dickhead! Why do you even care? Don't be such a loser. As if she even cares… you're putting too much importance on yourself.*

His phone pinged.

Ooh! Time for more dinners together. Maybe even a movie? Well… unless you're going away for the holidays.

Tom sat stunned, staring at the screen. *Did she just ask me out on a date? What do I say? Play it cool, Tommy. Play it cool.* This was why he didn't date! It was all too stressful. He wiped his palms on his shorts.

A movie sounds great! I thought you'd be heading home for Christmas with your family.

Those three little dots flashed. He was becoming addicted to her text messages. His paperwork, forgotten.

SIX

Standing in front of his wardrobe, Tom fretted over which shirt looked best with his blue jeans. Should he wear the T-shirt or the button-up? The T-shirt would look more casual but often highlighted his bulky shape. Tom screwed up his face, thinking about it. He snatched the dress shirt off its hanger, racing through the house to iron it.

He'd spent the day washing and polishing his beloved EH Holden sedan. Driving her always made him feel confident and boosted his self-esteem. He'd built her with wrecker-yard scraps and a lot of hard work. She was the most precious thing he owned. Driving her, he couldn't help but smile.

Collecting Lauren from her place, he revelled in her reaction as he pulled up. He didn't take her for a car person, but she seemed impressed. The sweet scent of her perfume once again filled the air between them in the confined space of the car, sending butterflies fluttering in Tom's stomach. He hoped it lingered on the leather seat she occupied. She always smelled amazing.

"So… *now*, will you tell me where you are taking me tonight?"

Tom's smile grew wide. "And ruin the surprise? Never."

He watched her roll her eyes with a smile tipping up her beautiful full lips before returning his gaze to the road ahead. He'd thought about her lips so often in the weeks past. Lips he longed to kiss and find out if they were as soft as they looked. He felt the bulge suddenly growing in his jeans and shifted himself in the seat. He stole another glimpse of her as she looked out her side window, and his eyes dropped to the part of her he loved so much. That spot at the small of her back where the skin led down into the backside of her jean shorts to that sexy, round peach of a rump. He wanted to bite that peach so badly.

Without warning, Lauren spun around, her mouth open to speak. *Shit!* Caught looking at her ass, Tom felt his face flush with guilt. She stared at him silently while he averted his eyes to the road. He wasn't sure if it was two seconds or two minutes that passed, but his focus remained riveted to the road. The awkwardness, palpable. He wanted to know what she was thinking but wasn't game to ask.

Was it only him, or did the air in the car suddenly feel electric? Was she angry with him? Should he try to explain, or would she see straight through his bullshit? Probably the latter.

"What were you going to say?" Tom tried to glide over the whole moment.

"After catching you checking me out... I honestly don't remember."

So she wasn't going easy on him then? He risked a peek at her and found a smug look entertaining her face. Evoking one of his own. "Okay. You got me. I'm sorry. For what it's worth... I was looking with admiration, if that makes a difference?" He wrung his hands against the polished steering wheel. He hoped his beard hid the blush heating his cheeks.

"It's fine. If we're being honest, I've been sneaking peeks at you, too. So, call it even?"

That got Tom's attention. "You? Have been looking at me? Why? That's hardly a fair trade. Your view compared to mine." Why did he say that? He wanted to bite his tongue off.

"What do you mean by that?"

Me and my big mouth! "No, nothing. Just that we're—" Tommy stirred the air between them with his hand. "Well… you're *you*. And I'm… well, this." *Stop waving your arm around, dickhead. You look ridiculous!*

From the corner of his eye, Tom saw Lauren's entire frame twist in her seat to face him square on. "Um… what do you mean you're '*this*'? You know… I think I take offense to the implication that who or what I want to look at is anything less than worthy of my admiration. I know what I like, and I like what I see."

Lauren crossed her arms. There was 'challenge' written all over her face. If Tom weren't so freaked out by the idea of her checking him out, he might have been playful enough to spar with her and draw out the feisty bumblebee again. However, with his thoughts scattered as they were, he gave her a half-hearted smile and returned his eyes to the road. *Thank god we're nearly there, I need to change this conversation to safer subjects.*

Pulling into the carpark, Tommy collected a ticket, found a parking space he liked and killed the engine. Unable to look at her and filled with tension, he opened his door to escape the awkwardness he felt.

"Hey?" Lauren's hand landed on his thigh and for a second, Tommy couldn't breathe. "I meant what I said. I really like you. And whether you believe me or not... I'm finding it more and more difficult to keep my hands and eyes to myself when I'm with you."

Tom finally looked at her then... into the purest blue eyes he'd ever seen. His heart pounded in his chest with such force, he hoped she couldn't see it. He swallowed hard, his lips pasty. When had his mouth turned into a desert?

The touch of Lauren's hand burned through his jeans. The heat sent sparks shooting through his veins like fireworks, awakening parts of himself he'd long chosen to extinguish.

Tongue-tied and in a panic, Tommy pushed his beefy frame up and out of the lowered vehicle, keenly aware of how chunky he must've looked.

SEVEN

Jacaranda Street was bustling with people. The pedestrian-only street was the thoroughfare that linked the large shopping precinct within the city itself. Waist-high garden beds adorned both sides of the walkway. People jostled to secure their places to watch the parade. Tom spotted a small section of empty garden bed and tugged Lauren by the hand to claim it. She smiled widely at him over their minor victory.

"Well done, good sir." Her praise hit him straight in the heart. He loved the warm feeling it stirred.

"Thanks." How was it he could text with her all day—and night—but as soon as she was in front of him, he clammed up like a damn teenager? He was a grown-ass man. *Think of something, idiot. You're choking here.* "So… I thought since this is your first Christmas in the big smoke that I'd bring you to the annual Christmas parade and then after that we can get a bite to eat or head over to South Pier and check out the Christmas markets, what do you think?"

"I think that sounds wonderful. Thank you for bringing me."

The sound of drums started rumbling up the top end of the road somewhere, catching people's attention. A brass band joined in, and excitement lit up Lauren's face as she turned towards it, stretching up on her tiptoes.

"Here," Tommy hoisted her up to sit on the thick concrete edge of the garden bed. Lauren, with the eagerness of a child, sat up straighter to see through the crowded patrons. With his arm tucked around behind her, he let his hand rest against her hip and backside. The feeling of her now reminded him of their moment in the car. Just like before, sparks ignited. Fireworks went off in the pit of his stomach.

The band moved closer. Children all around them stood high on garden beds and edging. Some sat high on dads' shoulders—anything for a better look at the festivities. Tommy adored how their little faces lit up in wonder as they spied the stilt people walking down the road amidst the parade spectacle. To see the dancers perform to the tune of Christmas carols. Tom could see himself one day being 'that dad' who would have his little boy—or girl—perched on his broad shoulders while Lauren stood beside him, smiling up at their chubby-cherub face. Perhaps she had the baby on her hip. What would their kids look like?

Tommy shook his head subtly and rubbed his eyes to clear the vision from his mind. What the hell was wrong with him? He couldn't dig up the courage to kiss the girl, much less give her babies!

"What's wrong?"

Tom looked up to find her watching him from her high vantage point, concern on her face. "Huh? Oh, nothing. Are you enjoying the parade?" he leaned up towards her ear so she would hear him over the band who'd begun passing them. He was still close when she turned to see him. Her eyes roamed his face. One eye, then the other. Her gaze dropped to his lips, and he heard her inhale before returning to stare into his eyes once more. It was the sexiest thing he'd ever seen. He'd seen it in movies plenty of times, but seeing her do it, and to him, of all people. Tommy felt electricity zing between them.

Tommy reminded himself of all the people and small children surrounding them. Ravaging her wasn't acceptable. His growing cock, however, had a hard time understanding that and wished he would forget all rational reasoning.

"You wanna go grab something to eat?" Tom thumbed over his shoulder. He needed a distraction, or he might disgrace them both, right there on that damn garden bed.

Lauren nodded in agreement.

They headed towards South Pier, where they would find something to eat and check out the Christmas stalls. They were making their way across the bridge when Lauren stopped to watch the boats moving about in the river beneath them.

"They're the ferries. I must admit, they're pretty impressive. They get up some solid speed in between stops. Have you ever seen them before?"

"Huh," Lauren observed them crisscrossing the river. "Gosh... so much more to see here than back home." She shivered as a breeze travelled up from the water below. Tom noticed the goosebumps prickled along her arms.

"Sorry. I should've told you to bring a jacket. I always forget how cold the city gets at night. Even in the summer. I have so much extra padding that I don't feel it like others do." He stuffed his hands in his pockets and shifted his weight to the other leg. "Come on, it won't be so breezy amongst the market stalls."

"I have a better idea." Lauren took him by the elbow and tugged his hand free from his pocket. "You could let me snuggle in against you and wrap your beautiful warm arms around me so I can warm up for a minute before we leave this pretty spot." She was such a tiny thing. The top of her head barely reached his shoulder. Standing so close, Tommy had to lean back to see her beautiful eyes. Their hue, hard to see against the dark of night.

With her arms folded up between them, she laid her head against his chest. Tommy closed his powerful arms around her protectively. *Can she hear my heart racing? Can she feel my fat belly? What is she thinking right now?*

"What are you thinking?" he blurted out, not sure if he wanted the answer.

"I'm thinking… I'm having the best night." Lauren wrapped her arms around his waist, pulling him closer.

Tom automatically sucked in his stomach and stretched taller, stressed she would learn just *how* big he was underneath his clothes. She squeezed him tighter. His brain split in half.

On one side, he loved the feel of her pressed up against him. To have her in his arms finally, he wanted to sear the memory of her into his brain and body to take home later and lay in bed thinking about while he drifted off to sleep.

The other side, however—the far more chaotic and noisy side—of his brain was screaming at him. *She'll be repulsed! Will she reject me? If so, will she do it here... publicly? No, she wouldn't. How well do you really know her, though? She's more genuine than that. I think.*

Tom swallowed. The anxiety stuck in his throat like that time as a kid when he'd gotten a giant gobstopper stuck in his mouth. His mother had laughed. With little sympathy, she'd told him he'd just have to keep sucking at it until it was small enough for him to pull out with his fingers. Advice that hadn't helped him then and didn't help him now. He closed his eyes above her head, trying to steady his breathing. *What will be, will be. If she doesn't like me... well, what can I do about that?* He told himself the words, but he knew his heart wasn't okay with that answer.

"Your turn. What are *you* thinking right now?" Her head swivelled skyward to see him, but her ear never left his chest.

"Me? Oh, ah, I'm not sure." He shrugged, afraid to share his insecurities. She had a way of seeing him. He felt vulnerable. Like she knew what he was thinking before even asking him.

"You must be thinking *something*. Come on. Tell me?" She shook him gently. She felt incredible, even if her actions were panic-evoking. How long had it been since he'd held a woman? Any woman.

The pressure of having to come up with an answer. Of course, he could think of nothing else to tell her. "Um… I'm thinking how incredible you are. How beautiful—"

"Tom? Tom, what's the matter?"

Heat flooded Tom's body, and the world began fading. Lauren was there, but she felt out of reach. He could no longer hear her. A heaviness overcame him, and he needed to sit down, but his body wouldn't cooperate. His limbs felt disconnected from his brain. Why weren't they working? *Oh shit.*

Everything turned black.

What the hell?! Tom opened his eyes, and confusion struck him. Where was he? *Lauren. I was with Lauren. We were… here… on the bridge. Where is she? Did she leave? Who are all these people? Why are they all looking at me?*

Realising he was lying down, and embarrassed in front of so many bystanders, Tom started getting up, only to stumble again. Soft hands guided him to sit, leaning him back against the railings. The cool metal was a welcome relief. *Why am I so hot? And sweaty? Where's Lauren?*

The soft hands returned and finally, when his eyes cooperated, he lifted his head and found her. Wearing a very distressed look. Tom tried for a weak smile, but he couldn't be sure if his face was complying yet. He watched as she pulled a water bottle from her bag and uncapped it. She nodded to someone, and some of the gathered bystanders moved off.

"Here, have a sip of water. Can you hold it?" Lauren's face was only inches from his. She gave him the bottle but kept her hands close, obviously not trusting his ability yet. Her eyes, pools of concern, stared down into his. Tom blinked.

"I'm sorry. I think I ruined our date." He leaned forward and rubbed his face; his arms were still heavy, but they were getting better slowly.

"You haven't ruined anything. All I care about right now is you. Are you alright? Do you faint often?" A man Tom didn't recognise tapped Lauren on the shoulder. If he had more strength, Tom would've told him to back off. Lauren returned her attention to him then. "Do you want us to call an ambulance?"

"Shit no. I'm fine!" Embarrassed, Tom waved the guy off. "We'll go and get you that dinner I promised you, hey?" He smiled, but even he heard the lack of conviction in his voice.

"I think we'll sit for a little longer. Let's make *absolutely* sure that you're good before we set off again, yeah?"

"Do you mind if we call it a night, actually? I think it might be better if I headed home."

"Of course."

Tom stood up slowly. Lauren helped steady him, hovering like a little mother hen. His beautiful bumblebee. Feisty as hell when they'd met, but tonight, she was the sweetest, purest honey he could've imagined. She was classic beauty, inside and out.

EIGHT

The night grew late. Tom's friend Pete came to their rescue when Tom wasn't safe to drive and learned that Lauren couldn't drive a manual. On Lauren's insistence, Peter delivered both Tom *and Lauren* to Tom's house. Peter parked the classic car safely away and took the work truck home after he and Lauren got Tom up the front stairs and safely inside. Peter gave Lauren his mobile number and instructed her to call him if she needed anything through the night, no matter what time.

"I can't believe you can't drive a stick." Tom muttered. He shook his head in disbelief. "My girlfriend can't *not* be able to drive a manual. I'll have to teach you. I thought everyone in the outback drove manuals!"

"Am I your girlfriend?"

With his glass of water halfway to his mouth, Tom froze. It had slipped out. Trying to think of what to say, he braved a look at her. He never got to reply. Soft, strawberry flavoured lips touched his. A brief and delicate kiss. He breathed her in and nudged her nose gently with his own, breaking the kiss. They sat, taking each other in. A small frown creased Lauren's forehead, and she dropped her gaze.

Am I that bad? Tom's heart sank, thinking of what could cause such a reaction.

"Tom… do you like me and you're just—I don't know—painfully shy? Or are you trying to tell me you aren't interested without *actually* saying the words? Because you're kinda giving me mixed signals here. I don't know how else to show you I like you. But if I'm wasting my time—"

"Shit. Jesus. No." Frustrated and tongue-tied, Tom shook his head and twisted on the lounge to face her squarely. He needed to get this right. He took a steadying breath and held her hands in his own bear paws. "I like you. A lot. I'm not good at this stuff. Growing up, all my friends were tall, fit, sporty types. They all got girlfriends, and I became everyone's *friend.* Being shorter than my mates was hard enough, but being built like a keg on legs, well—"

Lauren burst out laughing, covering her face with her hand. He could see she was trying not to laugh. Somehow… he didn't feel ridiculed. Not by her. For once, he knew she was just genuinely amused by what he'd said.

"Oh, my goodness. I'm so sorry! I did not mean to laugh just now. Truly! I have never heard that expression, and the image that popped into my head was funny. For the record… you are not at all a *keg on legs*, as you say. You are… strong. You are thoughtful and warm. And when you held me tonight—before you collapsed on me—you felt… safe. Like nothing could hurt me while tucked up in your protective arms. It felt…special. To me at least." Lauren trailed off.

Tom absorbed her words. "To me too." He began plucking at a loose thread on one of the couch cushions. "Before I went and crashed like an idiot. I'm sorry about that. I guess I probably gave you a bit of a fright, huh?"

"Um… kinda. What was that all about, anyway? Do you often faint? Will you see a doctor about it? Sorry, that's probably not my business."

Tommy shook her hands lightly. He needed to tell her; she would find out the truth soon enough anyway. "Lauren, there are some things you need to know. I don't collapse often, but I do occasionally." He opened his mouth to speak, but nothing came out. This was exactly what he had been avoiding all these years. People couldn't hack it when shit got real. It was just easier to avoid them all together. "When I said I'm not good at this stuff… well, I wasn't joking. Put simply… I was out in the roaring-hot sun all day with my car. I skipped lunch… and breakfast, and I was a bit anxious about tonight. Okay… I was a *lot* anxious. And then you hugged me, which just kind of… pushed me over the edge. Not… not that you did anything wrong! Shit!" Tom scrubbed at his face. "I'm saying this all wrong."

With a deep breath, he started over. "I have diagnosed anxiety issues. God, I hate those words. I could give you a fistful of deeper explanations, but to be honest… I don't want you to see me as a patient. As a quest for you to fix. Truth be told, it really freaked me out when you told me you were a psychology student. Yes, I have a few issues, but they're mine to deal with. And for now at least, I'd like to keep them to myself. I know that sounds awful, and I don't want to hurt your—"

"You don't have to explain yourself, Tommy. I would never push you to talk about or do anything you didn't want to. I want to share something with you, if I may?"

"Of course."

"I don't tell many people this, but I went into psychology because of my dad. He suffers from a range of mental health challenges, and growing up, it was hard. Hard to be around him. Hard to get any help for him because we lived in a tiny little town where everyone knows everyone's business. I knew I wanted to help people, even if it's only in a small way. I want to build a counselling and psychology service that focuses on people in remote and rural Australia, so that families and farmers like my dad have someone they can talk to. Someone they can confide in and who won't tell Bessie down at the butcher." She paused for a moment. "It sounds like you have a good understanding of your needs already. All I want is to be your friend—maybe even your *girlfriend*—I'd just like to be someone you can trust or lean on when and if you want to. How does that sound?"

"Are you sure you can handle being with someone who's *broken?*" Tom continued to fiddle with the thread. His eyes downcast.

"Hey, look at me. Tommy. Look at me." Tom's hands stilled.

Having her so close, this conversation, his anxiety was gaining again. Words failed him. He looked up into her beautiful eyes.

"Firstly, you are *not* broken. And secondly, we don't have to unpack any of this right now. I can see that you're working yourself up again, and I don't want to be a stressor. I'm not going anywhere, so we can talk more about *what we are* another time. At your pace, okay? She looked at him then. For acceptance, perhaps? He wasn't sure. "Tommy, it's totally okay if you aren't ready or don't want to, but may I please kiss you? Seeing as we missed out earlier."

An embarrassed chuckle escaped Tom, and air rushed from his lungs. *How long was I holding my breath?* He nodded and dropped his gaze to the floor briefly. The fear of not being enough for this angel amplified in his brain.

Feeling her breath on his face as she neared, Tom swallowed down the lump of uncertainty and delicately kissed her tender lips. The kiss grew into a deeper, more adventurous exploration of tongues and senses. Lauren let out a soft moan, making Tom's heart race, but this time with excitement. *She is so damn sexy.*

They shuffled closer. Tom cradled the back of her head, feeling her soft hair beneath his fingertips and stirring the fresh scent of her shampoo, adding to Tom's desire.

Her lips were soft and plump. Her tongue, like velvet, seeking and encouraging. He leaned into it, allowing himself to open up to her. His erection grew painfully large within the confines of his jeans. Trying to shift positions, he winced when something pinched. Lauren jolted backward, concern filling her eyes.

"Nothing. I. I just. Never mind." Tom waved his arm, brushing it off and blushing the colour of ripe tomatoes.

It didn't work. Ever astute, Lauren read the situation and quickly caught the reason for his fumbled embarrassment. With a quirk of her lips, she inched closer again. Her lips returned to his, sparking another round of passionate kisses. Tom felt her hand rest on his chest between them. The heat radiated through to his skin, leaving the rest of his body feeling neglected and cold. He shivered.

Lauren's hand inched lower. Tom instinctively sucked his stomach in, making it harder to breathe properly but unable to stop himself. He forced his thoughts back to her kisses and the scent of her sweet perfume and shampoo. Her hand fell to the hem of his shirt, where she slid it up inside the fabric. Tom broke the kiss, yanking his shirt down, and bumping her hand away in the process. Lauren, startled, pulled back, and Tom thought he detected hurt in her eyes before she dropped her gaze to the floor at her feet, a frown creasing her forehead.

Tom fled to the kitchen. Anywhere to escape those big blue eyes of hers. Leaning against the kitchen bench, he stared out the window and down to his backyard below. Illuminated only by the moon, he could hardly make out the trees. Only a handful of leaves hinted at their whereabouts; the rest, concealed by shadows. He wished he could hide away in the dark… just like the trees below.

He didn't want to hurt her or lie to her, but there were some lines he was incapable of crossing yet. He wanted to be bold… like his mate Pete would be. He wanted to scoop up her tiny frame and deposit her squarely in his lap so they could be closer. To have her soft hands all over his body as he let her strip him free of his clothing. Feel the heat of her most intimate parts through his jeans, tormenting his dick until he couldn't stand to be restrained any longer. To touch her there and tease more moans from her lips.

But Tom wasn't Pete, nor was he bold. He hated his body. To believe that anyone *else* could want him was a notion beyond his comprehension. Anyone who wanted Tom would have to move slowly and be painfully patient with him. Did such a woman exist? Could Lauren be the gentle influence he needed? His stomach twisted, and the more he thought about it, the worse he felt.

He heard her move in close behind him, but she did not touch him. He dropped his gaze down to the sink where his hands rested along its edge. With eyes closed, he sucked in a ragged breath, his stomach still doing cartwheels.

"I'm sorry," he said. "It has nothing to do with you, I swear. I just—" he struggled to find the right words. "I need a little time." He turned to face her finally. "Can you be patient with me? I know I'm hard work," he said dejectedly.

"Of course I can. I'm sorry I overstepped. I didn't realise there was a trigger there. You might need to be patient with me too. Just while I learn where the parameters lie. Will you help me? I want to learn, Tommy. I want to know you."

Relief moved through him slowly and with a lop-sided smile, Tom nodded. He reached out to her and gently stroked her cheek with the rough and calloused pad of his thumb. His giant hand dwarfed her delicate features. He kissed her with the softness of a feather. That was when he felt it. She leaned into his hand. His touch. It stirred his insides in a way he'd never experienced before. There was something powerful about her. She was different.

NINE

Seated at his desk in the grimy office that could only be that of a mechanic, Tom sat staring at his phone. A harmless, inanimate object just lying there on top of the pile of paperwork he was yet to deal with. How could such a thing bring a person so much joy, yet so much anxiety as well?

Despite his best hopes, things had gotten weird between him and Lauren after the night of their date. He'd dropped his defences, and she'd slipped in, leaving him off-balance and unsettled. Then, the whole fainting issue from years ago happened again. Of course, it had obnoxiously chosen *that* night to return. He needed to regain control of things, especially his damn body. But that wasn't as easy as it sounded. He wanted to call her.

But what should he say? He wanted to see her. But what would happen? What would she expect? Tom didn't know how to move past these crippling fears.

His self-sabotaging traits ran so deep, they weren't conscious decisions he made. They were Tom's normal, and he would have to fight against them if he wanted to be with Lauren. He felt like such a fool. A stupid fool who wasn't cut out for any of this. Why he ever thought he could be was a mystery. He knew he owed her an explanation. She deserved that, and so much more, but all he could do was sit there, staring at his phone on top of that pile of papers. He twirled his pen in his fingers, avoiding… life.

In the quiet space of his office, Tom allowed himself to briefly open the locked chamber of his heart and drift back into the memory of that night. The feel of her in his arms as they'd stood there on the bridge. The sound of the water moving below. Even the faint chatter of other people walking along the bridge enjoying the evening like themselves. The cool touch of her hand against his clammy skin as he sat dazed against the railings. The embarrassment he now felt when he remembered how dishevelled and bulky he was, sitting there like a rotund blob of sweat.

Moving past that specific memory, he let his mind wander to later that evening. How she'd looked sitting there in his lounge room. The way she'd looked at him with her striking blue eyes… as if he was someone special. The feel of her smooth and delicate cheek. Her soft lips. The look of longing he'd seen in her eyes right before he'd freaked out. He might've still had a chance with her but instead, he'd sealed himself back behind all of his walls, and fled under the guise of 'needing to shower,' and completely blown those chances! He'd wrecked the mood. And for what? They'd both known that he was running. He hadn't fooled her; only proven what a coward he was. By the time he'd returned, she'd fallen asleep on his couch, a cushion tucked beneath her head.

His phone rang.

Fuck! He'd stuffed up so badly. He buried his face in his hands angrily. She would be better off if he just disappeared from her life. She deserved better than all his baggage. He should just let her go. The thought left him feeling hollow. He blinked hard against the sting in his eyes and scrubbed at his face roughly before answering the persistent shrill of his mobile.

The day wore on, and Tom wondered if it would ever end. He locked himself away in his office, finally dealing with all the filing and administration duties he'd been avoiding. He didn't have it in him to face customers today. Jack and Pete knew what they were doing. When thoughts of Lauren's gentle hands crept back into his mind, he shut and locked the door on them and moved to another task. How long had it been since he'd seen his desktop? He couldn't even remember. A sticky old coffee ring stained the corner of the desk. He went to find a rag to wipe it over. He was heading back up to the mezzanine level when he heard Peter call out.

"Tommy… you okay?" Peter's voice carried across the shed with little effort. The tin walls making everything echo.

"Yeah. Good. Why… you need something?" Peter gave him a thumbs-up and went back to what he was doing.

Back inside his office, Tom scrubbed vigorously at the desktop, willing the stain to budge. The stickiness was gone, but the stain of the ring remained, taunting him. He would bring in some cleaning wipes tomorrow from home and see if that did the trick. A knock sounded on the office door. He begrudged the interruption.

"Come in."

"Hey—" Pete paused as he entered the room, looking around, clearly taking in the tidy transformation. "We're um…We're all finished up out here. Last customer just drove out. I've counted out the till and bagged it up. Did you wanna check it? Or just lock it up?" Pete held out the bag to Tom.

"Seriously? Of course, I trust you. Just chuck it in there, and I'll make sure I lock it before I head out. Thanks for doing that."

He watched Peter cross back to the door and stall. "Was there something else?"

"You sure you're all right? You seem a little off today. I just want to make sure everything's okay. This…" Pete waved his hand, indicating the office space. "Just looks a little familiar. You know?"

"Pfft. Are you kidding? You saw this place, right? It was well and truly past overdue. That's all. I should've done it months ago. See you tomorrow?"

Peter nodded to Tom with one last questioning look before taking off.

Finally. The day was done. He'd gotten his office completely cleaned, and everything was back in proper order. With a sigh of satisfaction, Tom locked up and headed home.

Stepping inside his house was like stepping into a sauna. Locked up all day, the air inside was humid and stuffy. He opened up all the windows to let in the early evening breeze that his high-set rental always caught. How long had it been since he'd cleaned the house?

Tom felt the familiar itch of anxiety clawing at him but quickly dismissed it. *That's not what this is.* Unable to fight the compulsion, however, he stripped out of his uniform, chucked on some old clothes and—avoiding his reflection in the bathroom mirror—dumped his work gear in the basket. Armed with scrubbing brushes, cloths and cleaning sprays, Tom set to work, polishing every surface like it'd insulted him. It was close to midnight when he'd finally burned himself out and flopped into bed, exhausted.

TEN

What day was it? Tom couldn't even remember anymore. He knew he should care, but he didn't. There were people who relied on him, but the thought carried little weight. He needed to get up. Go into work. How many days had he missed? Was it one? A week? He should eat something. He wasn't hungry. Only tired. He was so tired he thought he could sleep for a month and still want more. Rolling over, he hugged a pillow to his chest like a life ring and let his eyes close once more. *The boys will understand.*

His head pounded. He squinted against the pain of it as he rolled to his back. Dazed, and a little confused, Tom struggled to remember where he was or what time it was. The pounding resounded again, and he realised that there was an external thumping that matched the one bouncing around in his head. He staggered out of his bedroom with his doona wrapped around him, towards the commotion.

"Tommy. I know you're in there. Open up, bud."

Tom froze at Peter's voice. He sounded mad. Tommy had let him down again. He'd known he needed to go into work today, but he just couldn't face it.

"Tommy, come on, man. I don't want to *have* to call them on you again. You know I don't. But if you won't let me in, I'll have no other choice. I know you don't want that. So come on. Let me in. I got you, remember? We always show up for one another. That's how we're geared, yeah?" Tommy remembered the pact they'd made as teenagers, working on cars together and joking that their pact needed to reflect their love of cars, and gears had seemed appropriate.

Tommy clutched the doona tightly to his chest as he stepped towards the front door. He felt sick. How long had it been since he'd eaten or drunk anything? He couldn't remember. His hand was on the lock when Peter thumped again, making Tom jump. He snapped it unlocked and stepped back, as if it possessed the power to hurt him. "It's open," he mumbled half into the doona.

Tom turned back to the couch. He needed to sit down before he collapsed. Especially if Peter was about to yell at him. He heard the door open as his backside hit the lounge. His whole body felt heavy. Just holding his head up was draining. It fell against the couch back, his eyes closed. Why was he so tired? The heaviness was suffocating him, and he wasn't sure how to find his way out. Against his will, he felt a tear slide into the hairline of his temple. He swiped at it angrily with the doona. *Fuck this shit! I hate this! I hate you! You're a useless fat fucker. Nothing more!*

His unyielding tears refused to obey, leaving wet tracks down the sides of his face. One rolled into the crevice of his ear; cold, it prickled his skin. Tom choked out a ragged breath as he fought to hold himself together, mentally and physically. To let go, the pain inside would surely rip him apart. The couch beside him moved, and he felt himself pulled into Peter's arms in an awkward sideways hug. He hated anyone seeing him this way. He knew Peter didn't judge him—they'd been through too much together—but it still made him feel weak knowing he was like this at all. Tom felt so stuck. To cry, really cry… felt like he would never stop, but to remain stoic felt like the weight on his heart would crush him to death. All he could do was exist. He couldn't breathe properly. He couldn't keep his thoughts straight. How was this supposed to get any better? He couldn't take anymore.

"I got you, Tommy. I'm right here. God, I'm so sorry, bud. I knew you weren't good the other day. I shoulda fought harder for you to open up then. Maybe this wouldn't have happened if I had. I got you. We're gonna do this together, okay? I always got you."

"I fucked up, Pete. Just like I always do. I fucked it all up. I've made a mess of everything with Lauren, and I really liked her, Pete." Tom broke down. His heart was tearing into pieces, and there wasn't anything he could do but endure the pain of it slicing through his chest.

"Tommy, god... I wish you'd come to me. You haven't... that's just it! Lauren's been worried sick about you. She's been texting me nonstop, asking me what she can do to fix this. She wants to be with you, bonehead. You just got all up in your head and didn't give any of us a chance to help you see it. Tommy, open your eyes, bud."

Tom wiped his eyes roughly with the edge of the doona, trying to pull himself back together. Reluctantly, he blinked a few times and sniffled hard. Was that a figure he was seeing on the opposite couch? He squinted, his eyes fuzzy from the doona and the darkness beneath it. *Oh jesus, please, no! Please don't let this be happening right now. Let a sinkhole open up and swallow me, couch and all! This can't be happening.*

Tom sat up, away from Peter, and pulled his arms up over his head, cocooning himself within the blanket. "Fuck, fuck, fuckity fuck. This is not happening. This *can't* be happening right now," he muttered. She was here?! *Why didn't Pete lead with that? Why didn't he say anything? Before I blubbered like a baby and looked like a complete loser.* Now he definitely needed the earth to suck him down to its fiery core.

"Dude, how could you not tell me she was here? I can honestly never come out of this doona now! Like... forever!" Tom cringed.

"Don't be silly. You know you have to come out of there. Who's gonna bail me out next time I'm strung up by that pack of mongrels again?" Tom heard Peter chuckle, but he knew it was hollow. Pete was forever looking over his shoulder and trying to keep one step ahead of his past. He made light of it now, but the threat he faced was very real. Tom drew strength from Peter's ongoing courage to face his life every day. He poked his head partially out of the doona, freeing only his eyes. His gaze darted between his pair of conspirators, unleashing their united intervention on him. He wasn't sure he was strong enough to face it all. To even face them. Since the night he cowardly ran from Lauren, he'd ignored her texts and dodged her calls. He didn't know how to make that back up to her. As for Peter, how many times was Pete going to have to pick him up and dust him off? Pete was the one being hunted, and here was Tom, falling apart. They were all better off without him weighing them down.

"What's going on in that big brain of yours?" Pete shifted on the lounge.

Tom's mouth felt glued shut. He didn't know how to talk. What to say. Where to start. He just shook his head and clung to the doona tighter. Peter and Lauren exchanged glances.

Peter smacked his knee. "Right... I'm going to make us all a cup of coffee. I know I need one, and I'd bet you haven't eaten in god knows how long, Tommy. I'll see if I can hunt down some biscuits or something." Tom witnessed another exchange of glances between Pete and Lauren before the lounge beneath Tom shifted as Peter rose towards the kitchen. The sound of water running and gurgling down the sink echoed through the otherwise silent house. Pete was rinsing out the kettle. How long had it been since Tom had showered? *I really should do that. I probably stink like death.*

Lauren rose from her seat across the lounge room, snagging Tom's attention. She moved in the slow, quiet manner that one might use to approach a wounded animal in need of help. *That is probably exactly how she sees you right now, dumbass.*

Tom hated the way she looked at him. Like he might shatter if she rushed. *Shit. I must look worse than I realise.*

"Tommy," her mouth opened and closed again several times.

Glad I'm not the only one who's tongue-tied.

She started again. "Tom. Please. Tell me what I can do to make this right. I just want to help you. Not as a therapist. As your friend and someone who cares about you. I want to be with you, but I don't want to overstep your boundaries, so I need you to help me understand what you need. Will you let me be here for you? I'm so sorry I pushed you too far the other night." Lauren's eyes dropped to her fidgeting hands in her lap. "I never meant to hurt you," she added before falling silent.

Tom reached for them automatically, covering them with one of his own. She met his gaze.

"You never hurt me. You never did anything wrong." Tom's throat was croaky with emotion.

"I must have. It was only after that night that everything went a bit... well... shit."

"No." Tom dropped the doona, shaking his head vehemently. "It was *all* me. I freaked out. That's what I do. I'm... Look, I'm not *the cool kid.* I never was. Everyone else just kinda *got it*, but I didn't. I'm not confident or *smooth*—"

"Yeah, you are. He is. Get him in a car and he's got some of the smoothest gear changes you'll ever find in a human." Peter interjected, placing down two cups of steaming hot coffee before disappearing again.

Lauren leaned towards Tom then. "I was the class nerd. With bracers *and* glasses. Trust me, I know that feeling," she whispered.

Her admission shocked Tom. For a moment, he wondered if it was a lie to make him feel better. Pete reappeared, and Lauren leaned back, a wink and a smile playing on her lips. Rattled, Tom turned his focus to Peter. He was carrying his own cup of coffee and a packet of *Digestives*?

Oh jesus. Is he trying to kill me? Why did he bring those out?

"You're seriously low on food, bud. Think we might get you some groceries before we leave. These are all I could find."

Yep… kill me now! They're digestives, alright. Tom moved to explain, snatching one up to demonstrate. "I don't have digestion issues or anything. I just like them, you know? The chocolate they use on the back melts nicely in the coffee. See?" He looked up from his cup to find Peter staring at him like he'd grown a second head. Tom stopped dunking. *You're such an idiot!*

Lauren smiled. "They remind me of when I was little. Growing up on a farm in the middle of nowhere, chocolate *anything* was rare. My nanna though," she pulled one from the packet and stared at it like she was back there. "She always had these in her cupboard. So, whenever we made the trip to visit her, I knew I was going to get two. *One for each hand,* she would whisper, before gently tapping my nose with her pointer finger and shooing me out of her kitchen." Lauren smiled fondly. Firstly at the biscuit, and then at Tom.

Her shared memory soothed something in Tom, and he relaxed a little. Together, they drank their coffee and made a plan. Tom was to shower and freshen up and, in the meantime, Peter and Lauren agreed to give him space and go buy a few groceries for him.

"I'm taking your keys, though, Tommy. We've been here before... You know?" Peter side-eyed him, and Tom nodded reluctantly. Pete's meaning was clear. *Don't try locking me out like last time.*

ELEVEN

With them gone, Tom sat on the shower floor, the hot water streaming down on him, fogging up the bathroom. He tried to analyse how he felt. What had gone wrong? He had no answer. He felt... detached. A somewhat comfortable numbness; like that feeling when circulation has been cut off to an arm or leg for too long. Beyond the pins and needles stage, you know it's still attached but there's no feeling in it. The pain is going to be awful once the blood flow starts again and the prickling knives overwhelm you; but you know you must go through it to come out the other side. To get back to 'normal.'

Tom sighed. The journey back to that better place would be long and exhausting. Would Lauren stick around? Could he pull himself through it all again? What alternative was there? He leant his head back against the tiled wall and took a steadying breath. *One step at a time. God, I hate those words!* With a groan, he stood and washed himself. His limbs felt even heavier than before.

Exiting the bathroom, Tom roamed the small house aimlessly, trying to find something to do with himself while waiting for the others to return. Fortunately, it didn't take them long, and he held open the door once he heard the car pull up.

"Ah, there's our man. You look brighter already. Got more colour in your face now. How do you feel?"

Tom's cheeks heated when he noticed Lauren studying him. What was she thinking? He gave her a shaky smile as she headed towards the kitchen with groceries.

"Yeah. Bit better." It was a lie. He felt horrible. Unsteady and overwhelmed by the continuous barrage of negative thoughts racing through his head. He wanted to scream at all of them and shut them off, but that is the thing about depression; it doesn't care about its host. It takes hold like a cancer, growing, infecting every part of one's life until there is nothing left. Just inky blackness everywhere. How did he tell someone that, though? He couldn't.

At that moment, Peter wrapped his arm around Tom's shoulders, interrupting his dark thoughts. "I know you're overwhelmed. I know you're all up in that head of yours right now, but we got you, alright. We've been here before, and we've made it out the other side. We will do it again. Just gotta keep breathing for me, yeah?" Peter gave him a slight shake—a display of brother-like affection.

Tom wiped away the moisture loitering on his lower lid. He wanted so desperately to believe his best friend, but in that moment, Tom couldn't see how any of this was going to be okay. He was everything he didn't want to be. Spinning tyres, twisted chassis. A passenger of his own making; powerless to stop it and about to wipe out everyone he loved before it was over. He'd lost control. He was...

Skidding sideways.

"I was going to make us all a sandwich, but then I realised I don't know what you guys like, so instead, I've made a mixed assortment. Can I get you guys a drink?" Lauren placed down the plate of colourful triangles, pulling Tom from his thoughts.

Without wasting a second, Peter jumped in. "Please. I would absolutely love a Diet Coke if there's any ice cubes in the freezer, but if not, water's fine, thanks. These look amazing. What about you,

Tommy? Have a Diet Coke with me? Or would you prefer water?" Tom knew Pete's angle… He wanted to see Tom eat and drink something. Both of which were the last things he felt like doing. There was no point in arguing, however. Doing so would only delay their leaving.

He knew he should drink water. He was no doubt dehydrated, but if anything was going to tempt him to drink, it would need to be sweet. "I'll have a Diet Coke too, please, Lauren. There should be ice cubes in the freezer. Top shelf, in the blue ice cream container."

Lauren returned, three full glasses of soda balanced in her hands. Pete jumped up and relieved her of one before she crossed to Tom. When his large hand wrapped around the glass, it was inevitable that their fingers would touch. Fireworks went off in Tom's stomach, making the idea of eating anything even more perilous.

"What's grabbing your attention, Tommy? Which sandwich do you think you're gonna go for? Do you want to start with only a half one first off? You haven't eaten in goodness knows how long, so I know you'll want to take it slow. I get that."

She was quick to correct it, but Tom noticed Lauren's frown of confusion before it disappeared. He contemplated explaining his quirky digestive system to her, but he just didn't have the energy for it.

Pete was overenthusiastic as he inspected the plate and all the different choices on offer. "What've we got here, Lolly? Looks like we've got some ham and cheese. Some plain salad ones, and is this ham and salad over here?" Pete pointed to a triangle without touching it.

"Um, yes. Except those are actually ham, cheese *and tomato*. But I can make a plain ham and cheese if either of you don't like tomato. Well... of course, I can also make you any other combo you like."

"Nuh, these look awesome. We're both pretty easy to please in the flavours department. There's not much that we won't eat. Both grew up with mums ready to clout us if we didn't eat what we'd been given," Peter chuckled. "What'll it be, Tommy?"

Tom shuffled forward in his seat, uncertain. Not only by the sandwich choices, but also by the two sets of eyes staring at him. Glancing between Peter and Lauren, Tom suddenly felt like an outsider. How long had Pete been calling Lauren *Lolly*? When had they become so familiar with each other? He frowned, trying to shake off the uncomfortable thoughts. Collecting a plate, he reached for a ham, cheese and tomato triangle. There was no way he could tackle all that salad with both of them watching him like a pair of tourists at the zoo. He knew they meant well. He knew they just wanted to help him, but he just wished they'd go home and leave him alone. *Would I really eat anything if they left, though?* He knew the answer before the thought passed. Of course not. With an inward sigh, Tom took a bite, trying to swallow it down without gagging. His stomach never played nice once he'd deprived it of food for any length of time.

TWELVE

The next morning, Tom woke groggy and confused. His head pounded. *How long have I been asleep? What day is it?* He reached for his phone on the bedside table, except it wasn't there. *What the hell? Where is my damn phone?* The memory of yesterday emerged. Pete and Lauren. He'd fucked up, and they'd called an intervention on his arse. He let his head flop forward back into his pillow, only making it pound harder.

He replayed visions of Lauren in his mind. How she'd looked at him when he finally came out of the doona. When she'd told him she was a nerd in school. The wink she'd given him. Even amidst his darkness, she'd had the power to light a spark in his heart. He sighed heavily.

He should let her go. A bright soul like hers should shine without being dampened by someone like him. Could he do it, though? Yes... he would do it for her. Even though just the thought of it was crushing him, she deserved so much more than he could ever offer her. He covered his face with an arm. With his emotions fractured, dark thoughts and negativity kept throwing him offtrack and sending him down destructive spirals. He needed to get up, go in search of painkillers.

Turning into the kitchen, Tom froze. In front of him stood Lauren, wearing one of his T-shirts. It was enormous on her tiny frame, covering her perfect peach of a backside. She was leaning over the sink, on her tip-toes, looking at something through the window. Even as short as she was, she was all legs in his shirt. He wondered if she had anything on underneath. *Don't be a creep!* He cleared his throat, announcing his arrival. He'd half expected her to jump. Instead, she merely turned her head, resting her chin on her shoulder. A soft smile, lighting up her beautiful face. She looked so angelic with the early morning sun streaming in the window behind her.

"Good morning. How'd you sleep?" she asked, searching his face for what, he wasn't sure. A sign that he wasn't about to leap from the window next to her? That he wasn't about to have another blubbering breakdown?

"I was about to make myself a cup of tea. Did you want one? Or coffee?" She was throwing him a lifeline. He wanted to take it. But hadn't he *just* decided it was best for her if he let her go? *Soon. I'll end it soon.*

"Coffee sounds great. Thanks."

Watching her move around in his kitchen like she'd lived there all along stirred Tom's insides. There was something comforting about it. He liked seeing her there. *Forget it, Tom! This is a dead-end road. Don't make it any worse on yourself.* "Here, let me do that. I should be offering you, not the other way around." Tom took the kettle from her as she finished filling it. Resting it on its base, Tom clicked the switch and retrieved two cups from the overhead cupboard. Reaching for a teaspoon, he paused, realising he didn't know how she took her tea. Did she have sugar? Milk?

He was staring blankly into the cup when Lauren moved in beside him and gently took the spoon from his hand. She was so close he could smell her shampoo. She smelled wonderful… like summer fruits. How did she wake up smelling so good? His mind was warring, which only added to his confused and spiralling state. Part of him wanted to lean into her. To take her in his arms and gently caress every inch of her skin while they lay together pretending to watch movies all day. The other part of him, the anxious part, wanted to jump back away from her nearness. To run from her before she saw the mess that he was and leave him alone, with the certainty of knowing that he had caused this. That he was unlovable. Just like his father had always said.

Outwardly, Tom found himself paralysed. Unable to advance *or* flee from her. His brain shooting him down dark tunnels left and right, he was stuck staring down into the empty cup while his thoughts ate him alive.

"Tommy?" she laid the spoon down on the bench soundlessly and collected his hand in hers. "Hey. I'm here. I want to be here. Pete and I have been talking, and he's filled me in on… a few things." Lauren shook his hand softly and despite all the noise in his head, Tom realised that *this* was her thing. Whenever she was trying to break through to him, she shook his hands. Somehow, she always seemed to know when his mind began pulling at his attention. She always knew when he needed help to return to the surface. "Look at me, Tommy."

Seeing her face. Looking into her blue eyes with those dark outer rings around them. He hated the pity he saw there. It was always the pity he hated most. He didn't want to be *weak*. He needed to toughen up. Everyone else was just getting on with their shit. He needed to do the same.

"Lauren, I appreciate everything you've done for me, but I think it'd probably be best if you go now," Tom said. Yes, this was the right thing to do. He stepped back, removing his calloused hands from her soft ones. A cold emptiness prickled his skin, cutting a path straight to his heart. He let it settle there, knowing it would hurt less if he locked away his feelings and squashed them down so deep they would surely suffocate.

"No, Tommy. I know you don't mean that. That's not you—"

"I do. I'm really sorry. The timing is shit, but I need to work on myself right now, and I can't do that if I'm always second-guessing what *you're* thinking as well. I'm sorry, I thought I could make this work, but I can't. I never meant to lead you on… but now, I'd like you to leave, please."

Tears filled her eyes. It was too much for Tom to bear, and he turned away, retreating to his room while listening to the sound as she gathered her things. Finally, he heard the front door close and her little car tear away down the street. Only then did he flop onto his bed, the springs groaning in protest. Wrapping himself up into a tight ball, he let his heart break wide open and wept for the woman and the relationship he knew he would never have. It was the fairest thing that he could do for her.

THIRTEEN

Returning to work felt like trudging through freshly poured concrete. Every step took effort. Tom worked robotically, doing the jobs that needed doing. His obsessive need for control and order no longer plagued him. Now in its place was the internal storm of this latest depression spiral where he sat amongst the rubble and the rain in his mind and heart. His entire being felt battered. Broken.

Tom did his best to avoid the workshop floor. He felt Peter's eyes on him everywhere he turned. Checking up on him, making sure he was eating and using any excuse to come into the office and scope out the space. Tom knew he meant well. Peter had been through all of this before with him. He knew what Tom was capable of, and he was doing everything he knew how to prevent another incident. Tom had no one to blame but himself for this overprotective behaviour.

Stuffing his laptop into his backpack, Tom jumped when a knock sounded on his office door. Peter's face appeared.

"Hey, I'm headed down to The Corner Cafe to grab something to eat. You want anything?"

"Nuh, I'm headed out for an appointment shortly, so I'll grab something then. You'll be okay to lock up for me tonight? Or should I head back here after I'm done?"

"Nope, that's too easy. Personal appointment or a work one?" Peter asked. Tom saw straight through his casual tone.

"A shrink, if you must know!" Tom grimaced. He hadn't meant to yell. "Sorry. Apparently, there is some new guy in town, and he has some vacancies or whatever, so he could fit me in. You know… 'cause I need to see someone immediately, apparently. I hate meeting new 'professionals'," Tom air quoted. "Always think they know what you need after spending an hour with you. Makes me a little crazy."

Peter nodded in agreement but made no move to leave.

"Was there something else?"

"Um… Lauren tells me you aren't returning any of her calls or messages. She's really worried about you, Tommy. Perhaps you could call her? Let her know how you're doing."

"Oh really? What else did she tell you? Good to know you've got my back! Maybe you pair should hook up so you can both play footsies in person and crack jokes all night long about your lame-ass friend Tommy who can't keep his shit together! I'm sure you could show her a real good time. You always were a smooth mover, able to have anyone you wanted!" Without another word, Tom launched from his chair and raced out the door, flinging his backpack over his shoulder as he went.

In the work truck, Tommy slammed the car into gear with so much force, it was a wonder he didn't snap the stick. Laying rubber down, he escaped the workshop. His hands shook with his rage while his fingers clenched the steering wheel with a white-knuckled grip. His heart was pounding. Who was he angry at? Despite his outburst minutes earlier, he knew it wasn't Pete he was angry at. Was it Lauren? No, he could never be angry with her. Himself? Maybe. But that didn't feel entirely right either. So who then?

"Shit! Stupid, stupid, stupid shit!" Tom thumped his hand against the steering wheel.

On the passenger seat beside him, his phone lit up with a call. 'Pete' flashed on the screen. He couldn't answer it. What would he say? He'd been completely out of line. For the first time ever, Tom was glad to have the old junker truck with zero technological features, so he had a valid excuse for not being able to take the call. Pete knew the truck didn't have hands-free capabilities.

By the time he arrived at the doctors' rooms, Tommy had several missed calls from Peter, two from Lauren, and a dozen messages. He couldn't deal with them now... his head was swimming as it was. Knowing he had to go in and play nice with some young, fresh out of university, no life experience, little punk, who would then charge him three hundred dollars for the privilege. *You need to stop thinking about everything. You're gonna have a heart attack, and that would suck after you've just handed over your three hundred bucks to this twat.* He slammed the truck door and locked it with the key.

Despite his early mark from work, Tom was exhausted by the time he reached home. As he'd expected, he'd recapped his entire life story to this latest therapist. Getting to know and build a rapport was always a tiring and tedious process.

In the kitchen, Tom had just finished pouring himself a glass of water when there was a pounding on the door. *What the hell?* He'd not heard anyone pull up, much less walk up the stairs. He'd barely reached the lounge room when more thunderous knocking came. Annoyed, he swung the door wide to find a red-faced and frowning Lauren staring at him with something resembling pitchforks in her eyes. She shoved him back, forcing her way past him.

"Oh, please do come in." Tom gestured with an arm in agitation and rolled his eyes.

"Don't you put this on me! What else am I supposed to do? You won't answer my calls or reply to my texts. And then Pete rings me this afternoon and tells me you insinuated that he and I are shacking up together. What the bloody hell, Tommy?"

"Should."

"I beg your pardon?"

"I said you should. Not that you were. Good to see he used a little *artistic license* with my words," Tom muttered under his breath while rubbing his forehead with his hand, an ache suddenly growing behind his eyes.

"Oh, my mistake. To be honest, I was finding it hard to concentrate on his words because my fury with you was maxing out at the time!" She unleashed her tirade on him, fists clenched at her sides. "Look, Tom, I know you're having a shit time of it at the moment. And you want me out of your life—" Pools formed in her eyes, and Tom saw her lip tremble before she shook it off and continued. "But I can't believe you would ever think I was capable of such a thing. I thought you knew me a bit better than that." She sniffled and swiped angrily at a tear trekking down her cheek. Tom's heart snapped seeing her like that.

"Lauren—" he reached for her.

"Just don't." She shook her head and stepped back, defeated suddenly. "And give Pete a call. He's been worried sick that you've done something stupid since you screeched out of the driveway today." She turned and left, leaving him standing in his front doorway alone as she ran back down his front steps.

"Lauren, wait." She kept going. "Where's your car? How'd you even get here?" He searched the street, looking for something to say other than what he really wanted to. He couldn't tell her how he really felt. Didn't she realise he wasn't good for her? That it wasn't fair on her to have to be bogged down with all his crap. He watched her walk up the street. All of her previous fire gone. She looked worn out and all alone. "At least let me drive you home!" he shouted, but she never turned around.

FOURTEEN

Watching Lauren round the corner and disappear was the jolt Tom needed to make his brain work. *What am I doing? Keys! Where are my keys?* Tom jumped into action, retrieving the essentials before heading out the same front door he'd watched Lauren barge through less than five minutes earlier. Pulling it shut behind him, it was about to latch when he remembered his busy day... he probably stank. A quick sniff confirmed his thoughts, and he raced back inside towards the bathroom.

With the speed of a man possessed, he stripped off his shirt and madly washed up in the hand basin. His mind drifted to 'what if's', and he brushed his teeth as well. In his frenzy, he rammed the toothbrush into his gum, leaving him cursing through a mouthful of minty froth.

Tom darted back to his room, leaving the rest of his discarded clothing strewn where they fell. Zipping up clean shorts, Tom reached for his keys once more and took the stairs at a run. Diving into the work truck, he spun the old girl's wheels for the second time that day and sped towards her house.

Tom scoured the sidewalk along the way in case she hadn't yet made it home. He didn't want to miss her. As her unit block came into sight, he spotted her checking her letterbox. He skidded to a halt on the kerb. Killing the engine, he left the keys hanging from the ignition and the driver's door wide open as he rounded the bonnet of the car.

With all her previous bravado now gone, Tom advanced towards her but stalled when he saw a hint of resignation—or was it fear—in her eyes? He couldn't tell, but the last thing he ever wanted to do was scare her. With measured steps, he closed the space between them. Close up, he saw the frown crease her forehead. Knowing he'd caused that frown wounded Tom. He hated knowing that he'd hurt her. He needed to make this right. But how? What should he say?

Thoughts rattled around in his mind. He stood there staring into her eyes, unsure where to start. Time seemed to split in half, both standing still but also racing ahead as well. He couldn't just look at her face all night. Everything had been so clear as he'd stood on his front landing watching her disappear, but now, here in front of her, he wasn't sure he could do it. Expose himself and hand over the keys to his heart? He panicked. Whoever held the keys held the power to either keep him steady or run him off the road and turn him into an unsalvageable wreck.

"Lauren, I—" Tom shuffled on his feet. His hands grew slick, and he wiped them on his shorts. He growled, consumed by his own frustration. "I'm not good at this. What I said to Pete… it wasn't a reflection on you. Or Pete, for that matter. It was me. My insecurities. I see that now. And I am deeply sorry for any pain I've caused you because of it. I just… I'm not good for you, Lauren. You could have anyone you want." Lauren opened her mouth to speak. "No, please… Let me get this out. I don't want to bog you down or drag you into all my bullshit issues. What if one day, years from now, you end up realising that you've wasted all your time on me and end up resenting me for stealing the best parts of you? I couldn't bear the thought of you ever hating me like that. I'm not sure I would survive it."

Tom's voice trailed off to a whisper. His shoulders slumped.

"Is it my turn now?"

Tom only nodded, unable to meet her gaze. "I've heard you say you don't think you're good for me. I've heard you say you don't want me to resent you years from now. I've heard you say you don't want me to get bogged down in your 'shit'—as you call it—I've heard you say that you're not cool enough for me and that I could have anyone I want. Tommy... I don't know how many more ways I can say this... I want *you*. All of you. Even the parts of you that *you* don't like. The shy parts, the messy parts, even the shit parts. My heart is already all in. Yep, I know that's scary. It scares the hell out of me too, but apparently my heart doesn't care if you think you're bad for me or not. I guess the question here isn't about what is right or wrong. The only question left to ask is... what do *you* want, Tommy? Not 'what you think is best'. What do you *want*? If I'm not what you're looking for, I get it. It'll suck and I'll miss you like crazy but—"

"I want you too," Tom interjected. "I always did. I just got... stuck. You know? I get so stuck. I'm a mess, Lauren." He admitted.

"I can do messy. So long as it's with you, I think I can do just about anything. I don't need you to be perfect, Tommy… I just need you to let me in. In case you haven't noticed… I'm a bit into you, you know?" She bent slightly to see his down-turned face.

"I'm sorry. I never meant to hurt you. Nor *do* I ever." Tom met her gaze, searching her beautiful face for forgiveness.

The moment stretched on before Lauren's radiant but shy smile grew. Tom noticed the now familiar zing in the air that radiated between them whenever she was near. His heart began pounding in his chest. She'd always had that effect on him. "Please, Tommy… can I please, please kiss you right now? It feels like it's been forever."

With an awkward chuckle and a warm smile, Tom reached for her. Wrapping his thick, burly arms around her tiny waist, he tucked her squarely against him. She felt like home. Like a warm blanket in winter, the smell of rain after a hot summer's day. He never wanted to let her go.

Coming up for air, Tom looked deep into Lauren's blue eyes, and it clicked. The emotion he saw there was real. Pure. Why had it taken him so long to realise?

He rested his forehead to hers. "Want to go grab a bite to eat? Tyres are still warm." He nodded towards the truck with a grin.

"Why don't you come inside, and I'll fix us something here instead?"

Tom agreed. So long as he got more time with her—now that they'd shared their feelings and sorted through some of their feelings—he didn't care where they were, so long as they were together.

FIFTEEN

Lauren towed him towards her unit, their fingers interlinked. At her door, he released her hand, but she stubbornly clung to it, unlocking and opening up with her free one.

Her unit was small. They stepped into a modest but tidy living area with a small but functional kitchen towards the back that looked out over a pint-sized courtyard. A small round table sat next to the kitchen in what was supposed to be a dining area, tiny though it was. The table sported three mismatched chairs and clearly served as a workspace rather than somewhere to eat. Crammed with textbooks, papers and the laptop he'd seen her working on that first day at the garage.

"What would you like to eat?" Lauren asked, heading for the kitchen.

Tom followed her and leaned against the bench, watching while her peachy round butt hung out of the open fridge door. His dick reacted instantly, and he groaned, suddenly not interested in food at all.

Lauren's head popped up over the door, confused at his reaction. Tom saw the moment she figured out his train of thought when a sultry smile contoured her features. Without taking her eyes off him, she abandoned her inner-fridge searching and went to him, pressing her length against him. Her body felt heavenly, even as the edge of the bench bit into his hip. She searched his face for a sign of what? Stress, anxiety, consent? He wasn't sure. He nodded gently, trying to reassure her.

Lauren slipped one finger inside the waist of his shorts. With her eyes locked on his, she ran the finger from one side of his waist to the other, skimming the tip of his cock as it passed. Tom's head fell back with his arousal. When it made the return trip, Tom let out another groan and felt his cock bob against her touch. Pulling her tightly to him, he ground against her with his hardness, trapping her hand momentarily. His head was heavy, but when he lifted it, he saw desire burning in her eyes. With her eyes locked on his, Lauren removed her hand, and slowly popped the finger in her mouth.

"Fuck," was all he managed before he crushed her lips to his own, kissing her like his life depended on it. She was the sexiest woman he'd ever met, and she was his.

In a tangle of limbs, they made their way around the corner to her bedroom where they fell together, forcing their kiss to an end as they both broke out laughing. Somewhere in the back of his mind, Tom heard the destructive voice reminding him to be relieved that he had been the one to go down first, removing the risk of crushing her with his bulk. He ignored it and focussed on the feeling of her draped across his body, her fingers entwined in his hair against her pillow. Grinding his hips against hers, he let his hard length rub within the confines of his rigid jeans. He'd never wanted to be rid of his clothes so much in all his life.

His feet hung over the edge of the bed. He toed off his shoes eagerly, hauling Lauren up to straddle him. He heard her moan into his mouth, fuelling his desire further. Sitting up beneath her, he held her close and kissed the length of her neck. Her loose-necked shirt fell off one shoulder, exposing a black bra strap. Seeing it against her soft, pale skin lured Tom in. With slow movements, he pushed the hair back from her face before gliding his fingertips along the crease of her neck and slipping the bra strap from her shoulder. With lips and teeth, he nibbled along the hollow of her collarbone. Her hips bucked against him, and she let out a whimper as her head lulled sideways.

"You like that, baby?" Tommy whispered against her ear.

For good measure, he repeated the action, evoking the same response from her each time. Knowing he held the ability to stir her so deeply encouraged Tom to open up his heart, and let Lauren see the real him beneath all the walls he'd built.

He slid his hand down the back of her shorts. Relishing the swell of her backside, he gripped her firmly in his large palm as he ground himself against her. Tom felt the heat emanating from her core against his jean front, and together they were fire. White-hot fire.

Lauren tugged at his hair. Forcing his head back, she claimed his mouth in a hungry clashing of tongues. Her hands began roaming his back as he continued pulling her along the bulge within his jeans. A moan escaped her, louder this time. Her hands slid down the length of his back, clutching at his hips.

In her feverish state, Lauren's hand left their safe house and ran up the inside of Tom's shirt, cradling his waist. Tom froze unconsciously, and only a second later, he felt Lauren halt as well. She didn't move an inch. Her hands, her hips, everything stopped. Tom saw her eyes drift closed as she realised what she'd done. Tom's own followed, and he sucked in a ragged breath, uncertainty and fear trying to overpower him. Lauren drew back minutely, resting her head in the crook of his neck again. He heard her laboured breathing.

"Lauren. I… I—"

"I know… I wrecked it. I think I'll go grab us a glass of water." Her muscles tensed as she prepared to move off him. Tom couldn't think of anything worse than feeling the sharp sting of cold air hitting his body where her warmth had been in that moment. With his hand still firmly inside her shorts, he tightened his hold on her, forcing her to look at him.

"You didn't. *I* did. I froze. But… but I didn't mean to. It's going to take a while for some habits to change." Tom licked his lips, his mouth suddenly dry. She knew he was anxious. Tom could see it all over her face. He shook her gently, trying to reassure her. "Do you… do you want me to take my shirt off, or do you just want to… you know, feel my skin?"

Tom frowned. *She won't like what's underneath. Maybe it'd be better if she only felt my mass? It's harder to tell someone's body size just through touch, isn't it?*

"You already know I want you, Tommy. If I didn't, I wouldn't keep reaching for you and wrecking our *moments.* I want to kiss my way around every little dot, scar, and freckle on your body someday. But I also know this is hard for you. I've always said we'll move at your pace and that hasn't changed. I think I'm falling for you."

"I just want to make you happy. And I think I might've *already* fallen for you."

Grabbing his face in both hands, she pulled his forehead to her own almost roughly. "Can you honestly not feel how happy you make me? I think my *happiness* must just about be leaving a wet patch all over your crutch." She giggled and kissed the tip of his nose.

Tom chuckled once and drew a fortifying breath to steady himself. *She wants me. That's what matters.* He kissed her on the mouth, tightening his hold to keep her warmth firmly against his own. Still unwilling to relinquish his hold of her, he let his free hand move along the skin of her ribs and back where he found and unclasped her bra. Lauren broke the kiss, surprise etched all over her face.

"Where on earth did you learn to do that so well… Mister *I'm a loner, haven't had many girlfriends?* Hm? Is there something you're not telling me?" she quizzed good-naturedly.

"Why don't you stop asking questions and help me out of my shirt?"

Lauren's smile dropped as shock overcame her. Her gaze searched Tom's for answers. Understanding. "Are you… Tommy, are you sure? We can—"

"I'm sure." Tom swallowed to dislodge the wad of anxiety threatening to ricochet through him and leave him in pieces. "Just. Well. If you don't like what you see, or it kills the mood for you. Just tell me and I'll… Well. I'll put my shirt back on or something." Feeling vulnerable and exposed, Tom wasn't able to look her in the eyes any longer. He ducked his head, kissing the crevice of her neck. Lauren wriggled, trying to get free, but Tom wasn't ready to face her yet.

"Hey. I want to see your face." Tommy shook his head no, continuing to drop plucky kisses along her neck while hiding his burning—and likely scarlet red—face. "Tommy…" she continued to wrestle for freedom, and he knew he needed to let go.

"Hey." She tipped his face up to look at her. "Tommy, look at me, please," she whispered, and he finally opened his eyes. "I don't know who put all this stuff on you about your body, or maybe it has been an ongoing battle of your own making, but I think you are so freaking sexy I honestly can't think of anything else! Like, it's even interfering with my studies at this point! I can't wait to see, touch and taste all of you." Lauren bit her lip. Tom saw both lust and devotion in her eyes. Letting her go, he outstretched his arms behind him, leaning back to allow her better access.

She placed her hands on his chest and slowly let them track their way south over his shirt front. Her thumbs glided over his budded nipples. Down his ribs and circled his belly button hidden beneath the material. He sucked in a breath, and her eyes flicked to his, silently searching for permission. Tom nodded shyly.

At the hem of his shirt, she let her hands climb up inside the space. She moved slowly, deliberately taking her time, letting him adjust and helping him feel safe between steps. Lauren shuffled backwards and inched his shirt up by degrees, showering his bare skin with kisses. Tom watched her progress with an odd combination of fear and desire. He forced himself to focus on the feel of her feather-light lips against his skin. She searched and held his gaze from beneath hooded lids as she kissed his navel. His ribs. He broke first. Dropping his head back and closing his eyes, Tom felt her hot tongue circle first one nipple, then the other. His dick reacting instantly.

By the time he was completely free of the garment, they were both a frenzy of lust and limbs. Tom forced her arms skyward as he peeled her shirt up over her head. Her full breasts and the hint of pink nipple, a tantalising sight beneath her untethered bra, forced high. Seeing her feminine curves, accentuated as she stretched, was almost his undoing. Almost. He hadn't come this far to embarrass himself now.

They haphazardly discarded the rest of their clothes as desire overcame them. Rough, calloused fingers found warm, wet flesh. Soft, delicate hands clutched hard, hot man. In a meshing of tongues and skin, they drew each other to the edge of ecstasy before crashing over it simultaneously and riding out the residual waves together.

As their breathing calmed, their limbs grew heavy. Tom felt his eyelids do the same. How many times had he worried about this moment? The moment he finally found the courage to be naked in her presence—anyone's presence. The anxiety he'd endured about 'afterwards.' Would he be crippled by panic and make a stupid fool of himself? Lying beside her as he was, the idea seemed laughable. There wasn't anywhere else he'd rather be.

The lust. The hunger. The salacious thirst he'd seen running through her veins, hitting him in waves like a ripple effect on his consciousness.

"You know… for someone who *hasn't had many girlfriends*, you are frighteningly good at that," Lauren mumbled sleepily.

"I could say the same about you, my dear. Maybe we just needed the right person to bring it out in us. I can't speak for you, but I definitely think you've changed me. Maybe changed is the wrong word. You've brought out a different side of me. You've helped me face things I never thought I could." He hugged her tighter, and she snuggled into his touch. Tom saw the strange image of a cat curling up and purring contentedly in his mind. A smile crept across his face before he fell asleep, Lauren draped across his body like a human blanket.

SIXTEEN

Six months later

"**W**here's Pete? What'd you do with him?" Lauren said, poking her head out the front door, searching for him.

"I'm here," Pete grunted. "Jesus, Lolly... What the bloody hell have you got in here?"

Lauren laughed. "I honestly don't even know. I was just chucking things into any box or suitcase I could find in the end. Here, let me take it from you." She reached for it as he crossed the threshold.

"Not a chance are you carrying this heavy sucker, girly. Where do you want it?"

"Ooh, tread lightly, Pete. You've seen my little bumblebee when she gets her feisty on. I'd be careful who you're calling girly," came Tom's friendly warning.

"Nuh, she'd never do that. She loves me. Don't you, Lolly?" Pete grinned his cheeky boy smile at her, sweat dripping off his brow. Looking between the pair, Tom knew how lucky he was that his best mate and girlfriend got along so well. He watched Lauren poke her tongue out at Pete before bursting into laughter and smacking him on the shoulder.

"I'm going to get us something to eat. You," she pointed her finger at Tom's nose, and he snapped at it mockingly. "Haven't eaten since breakfast, and you've been busting your butt all day." She picked her way through the boxes towards the kitchen.

Tom looked around at the mess crowding his lounge room. Boxes and suitcases littered most of the floor.

"Where the hell are you going to fit all this stuff?" Pete whisper-shouted to him from the far side of the room.

"I heard that!" came Lauren's distant remark.

The two men chuckled, loving how easily riled she was. Pete stepped his way through the maze towards the couch—what was visible of it. "Seriously though, your house isn't that big," Pete repeated quieter.

"I have absolutely no idea. But we'll work it out. It's going to be so much better for us. Only having one lot of bills between us. Rent alone has been killing us both. If we're ever going to afford a place of our own, only paying one lot of utilities has to be a good place to start our saving."

"For sure! And it's not like she doesn't spend every night here already!" Peter smirked.

"Oh, shut up. She does not. Well, she didn't. She will now though," Tom laughed. Peter and Jack loved to taunt Tom about being an old married couple ever since they'd worked things out and officially started dating. Since then, he and Lauren had gone from strength to strength, and their bond had intensified quickly.

"*She will now,* what?" Lauren reappeared, carrying a plate of sandwiches. Their signature snack whenever the three of them were together or the two men were working, and Lauren was around.

"Nothing, bumblebee. Pete was just saying how great it will be now that we can start saving for our own place." Tom winked at Peter, and the pair of them smirked. Lauren squinted at both men suspiciously, not buying their story.

"And what about you, Pete… when are you going to find yourself a little miss someone to help you *save money for a place*?" Lauren used air quotes to emphasise her point. "I have a friend who'd love to meet you. I've told her a little about you during our classes together."

Peter choked on the mouthful of drink he'd just swigged. "Ah, no. No offense, Lolly... You know I think you're awesome and all, but there is no one on my horizon, nor do I intend there to be."

Tommy frowned, remembering the last time he'd seen Peter genuinely happy or even content. It had been too long. He wished Peter would take Lauren up on her offer. Go out with someone new and maybe find happiness with someone worthy of his complicated but loyal heart. Then perhaps he could forget about and leave his love for Elizabeth Mason where it belonged... in the past.

"You okay, babe?" Lauren stepped close to Tom, resting her hand against his chest as she looked up into his eyes. Tom didn't know how she did it, but it was like she could read his mind with just one look.

"Huh? Oh. Yeah... just thinking. Let's move these boxes off the couch, so we have somewhere to sit."

Lauren squinted at him dubiously. His swift change of subject hadn't fooled her. He made a mental note to fill her in later about the whole 'Pete and Elizabeth' history. It wasn't a topic to bring up now while Peter was around. Even after all these years, he still got twitchy whenever her name was mentioned.

Tom and Lauren ended up offering Peter to stay for dinner to thank him for all his help with the move. Tom felt so lucky to have such an amazing friend who, no matter what, would always be there for him. To now also have Lauren seemed like more than he was worthy of, but while she'd have him, he would never let her go again. It still crushed his heart a little whenever he remembered how close he'd come to losing her for good. He shivered. Lauren had become so interwoven in his life, Tom couldn't remember the time that he had existed before she came along and gave his world colour and depth. Meaning.

Standing together as they waved Peter off, Tom stood behind Lauren, his arms wrapped around her. He thought of all the things he wanted to give her one day. The big wedding. The fancy house they dreamed of. The children he'd imagined were theirs months ago at the Christmas parade.

They stayed that way as they watched Pete drive away. Tom nuzzled into Lauren's neck, and her head lolled sideways, allowing him access. A soft moan left her lips. Heat surged in his groin. It felt so good knowing that they wouldn't have to spend anymore nights apart. His house was now her house. His bed was now her bed. It was with that thought... he realised that was exactly where he wanted to take her.

"Come on my sexy little bumblebee. Let's go to bed, and you can boss me around with that feisty sass-mouth of yours I love so much." He wiggled his eyebrows cheekily. Her responding blush turned him on with equal measure to her sharp-witted tongue. He was completely smitten. He knew it. The boys at work loved giving him shit about the 'swoony look in his eyes these days', but the truth was... Tom was so in love, he didn't even care.

Thanks for reading *Skidding Sideways*. If you enjoyed this story, I hope you'll leave a review on Goodreads and the vendor where you purchased it.

For a glimpse at Tom and Lauren's future or to read Peter and Elizabeth's story, you'll want to check out the latest edition of *Dangerous Thrills*.

~

He didn't just steal cars... He also stole her heart

Elizabeth Mason has finally got her life out of the gutter and going in a respectable direction. So why does something feel like it's missing? Returning home to look after her ailing mother, Elizabeth is quickly drawn back into the dangerous world of stolen cars and fast money—a world she worked hard to escape. So why isn't she walking away?

They say 'time heals all wounds' but Peter Jones knows it's a lie. He's done his best to sober up and stay out of trouble, but he knows better than most that trouble always finds him. That's why he needs to do this one last job. To be free from his past he needs to finish what he started. There's just one thing distracting him...

Elizabeth Mason is back in town.

Want more?
You might like J.H. Nelson's debut novel
Upon Butterfly Wings.

~

Not more.
Not less.
Just different.

"The lights are too bright. I'm surrounded by drunks. Oh, and I'm wearing a dress! Can things really get any worse?"

Danielle has given up on the world. Being autistic makes navigating social events uncomfortable and overwhelming. Why won't her family just leave her alone to read her books in peace, where she is happy and life makes sense?

At his cousin's wedding, it isn't the happy couple that Kevin can't steal his eyes away from. It's the bride's sister. She isn't like the other girls he's met. Unable to get her out of his mind, Kevin is determined to know her better.

Their differences have drawn them together, but will they also be what tears them apart?

www.ingramcontent.com/pod-product-compliance
Lightning Source LLC
Chambersburg PA
CBHW020532120726
47904CB00003B/1041